She's Not Good for a Girl,
She's Just Good!

Written by Suzanne Hemming
Illustrated by Jacquie Hughes

First published in 2017 by Thea Chops Books
www.theachopsbooks.com

A catalogue record for this book is available from the British Library
ISBN 978-0-9957259-0-4

Printed in Great Britain by Doveton Press Ltd on FSC certified paper
TCB001

She's Not Good for a Girl, She's Just Good!

For Thea

There once was a girl, with a head full of curls,
whose daddy had taught her to throw.

They would practice all day, whether sunny or grey,
and even in Wintertime snow.

See when she was two, she had picked up dog poo
and thrown it as far as she could.

Her mummy cried, **"NO!"**
but her daddy thought,
"Oh, that throw was really quite good."

After washing her hands
(as good hygiene demands)
and agreeing to never touch poo,
(see the germs can't be seen
and it's not very clean:
it's simply not something we do),

the daddy said,

"Flo, when did you learn to throw?

You threw with incredible ease.

What else can you do,

can you run fast too?

I could teach you?"

and Flo said,

"Yes please!"

So Flo and her dad drove her mum a bit mad,
as they practiced and practiced all day.

But as Flo grew older, her mum couldn't scold her,

she'd just smile and

"Go Florence!", she'd say.

And so our young girl, with her head full of curls,
continued to run and to throw.

Till a boy from school (who's a bit of a fool!)

said, "**Hang on, doesn't she know?**

Girls can't throw,

the ones that I know,

mess it up or just drop the ball.

They hold it all wrong,

they're not that strong,

and they can't run

that quickly at all!"

Well Florence just laughed,

she said, "Don't be daft!

Whoever said that is just mad!"

The boy (who's called Frank)

gave a shrug and looked blank:

"It's just what I heard from my dad."

Then our sporty girl,

with her head full of curls said,

"That's not what my daddy said.

I challenge you fool,

today after school."

And Frank turned around and he **fled!**

So Flo took chase, curls all over her face.

She could run as a quick as a cheetah!

Frank was quite slow and with his face all a-glow,

gasped, **"I simply can't run one more metre."**

He yelled out, "Stop!", to his knees he did drop,

"I can see that my argument's thin.

Your challenge sounds fair, I accept,

when and where?

But know this: I think that I'll win!"

Once the challenge was set,

after school they all met,

as everyone crammed in the gym.

They'd run once round the hall,

and they'd each throw a ball:

the fastest and furthest would win.

"On your marks, get set, go!"

Frank was slower than Flo

and she beat him

by two seconds flat.

All the kids were enthralled,

as they then threw a ball,

and someone cried,

"Well look at that!"

Not a sound in the hall,

it was too close to call,

they all wished the gap had been larger.

Though Flo had thrown well,

it was too hard to tell

whether Frank had thrown just a tad farther.

Once they were sure
just a millimetre more,
was the ball that young Frank had thrown.
Flo jumped with joy,

"I'm a girl, you're a boy
and we're both winners,
as we've just shown!"

The crowd clapped and cheered,

but one boy just sneered,

"I suppose she's good for a girl."

The crowd all turned round,

no one made a sound,

as Flo pushed back her long curls.

"Hey there what's your name?
Don't you see we're the same?
Girls are equal to boys! Understood?"
Frank, holding up Flo's hand,
said, "Don't you understand?

She's not good for a girl, she's just good!"

The End